Cinderellis
and the Glass Hill

The Princess Tales

Cinderellis
and the Glass Hill

Gail Carson Levine

ILLUSTRATED BY Mark Elliott

SCHOLASTIC INC.

New York Toronto London Auckland Sydney
Mexico City New Delhi Hong Kong

ISBN 0-439-26503-7

Text copyright © 2000 by Gail Carson Levine.
Illustrations copyright © 2000 by Mark Elliott.
All rights reserved. Published by Scholastic Inc.,
555 Broadway, New York, NY 10012,
by arrangement with HarperCollins Publishers.
SCHOLASTIC and associated logos are trademarks and/or
registered trademarks of Scholastic Inc.

12 11 10 9 8 7 6 5 4 3 2 1   1 2 3 4 5 6/0

Printed in the U.S.A.   01

First Scholastic printing, March 2001

Typography by Michele Tupper

To Nedda,

zesty, kind, and true—

my dear friend.

—G.C.L.

BOOKS BY
Gail Carson Levine

Ella Enchanted
Dave at Night

THE PRINCESS TALES:

The Fairy's Mistake
The Princess Test
Princess Sonora and the Long Sleep
Cinderellis and the Glass Hill

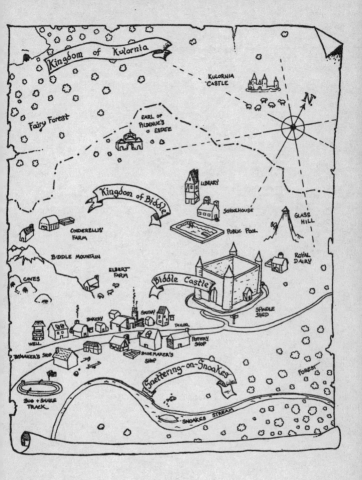

One

Ellis was always lonely.

He lived with his older brothers, Ralph and Burt, on a farm that was across the moat from Biddle Castle. Ralph and Burt were best friends as well as brothers, but they wouldn't let Ellis be a best friend too.

When he was six years old, Ellis invented flying powder. He sprinkled the powder on his tin cup, and the cup began to rise up the chimney. He stuck his head into the fireplace to see how far up it would go. (The fire was out, of course.)

The cup didn't fly straight up. It

zoomed from side to side instead, knocking soot and cinders down on Ellis' head.

Ralph and Burt came in from the farm. Ellis ducked out of the fireplace. "I made my cup fly!" he yelled. The cup fell back down the chimney and tumbled out into the parlor. "Look! It just landed."

Ralph didn't even turn his head. He said, "Rain tomorrow."

Burt said, "Barley needs it. You're covered with cinders, Ellis."

Ralph thought that was funny. "That's funny." He laughed. "That's what we should call him—Cinderellis."

Burt guffawed. "You have a new name, Ellis—I mean Cinderellis."

"All right," Cinderellis said. "Watch! I can make my cup fly again." He sprinkled more powder on the cup, and it rose up the chimney again.

Ralph said, "Beans need weeding."

Burt said, "Hay needs cutting."

Cinderellis thought, Maybe they'd be interested if the cup flew straight. What if I grind up my ruler and add it to the powder? That should do it.

But when the cup did fly straight, Ralph and Burt still wouldn't watch.

They weren't interested either when Cinderellis was seven and invented shrinking powder. Or when he was eight and invented growing powder and made his tin cup big enough to drink from again.

They wouldn't even try his warm-slipper powder, which Cinderellis had invented just for them—to keep their feet warm on cold winter nights.

"Don't want it," Ralph said.

"Don't like it," Burt said.

Cinderellis sighed. Being an inventor was great, but it wasn't everything.

∙ ∙ ∙

In Biddle Castle Princess Marigold was lonely too. Her mother, Queen Hermione III, had died when Marigold was two years old. And her father, King Humphrey III, was usually away from home, on a quest for some magical object or wondrous creature. And the castle children were too shy to be friendly.

When Marigold turned seven, King Humphrey III returned from his latest quest. He had been searching for a dog tiny enough to live in a walnut shell. But instead of the dog, he'd found a normal-size kitten and a flea big enough to fill a teacup. He gave the kitten to Marigold and sent the flea to the Royal Museum of Quest Souvenirs.

Marigold loved the kitten. His fur was stripes of honey and orange, and his nose was pink. She named him Apricot and played with him all day in the throne room, throwing a small wooden ball for him to chase. The kitten enjoyed the game and loved this gentle lass who'd rescued him from being cooped up with that disgusting, *hungry* flea.

King Humphrey III watched his daughter play. What an adorable, sweet child she was! Soon she'd be an adorable, sweet maiden, and someone would want to marry her.

The king sat up straighter on his throne. It couldn't be just anyone. The lad would have to be perfect, which didn't necessarily mean rich or handsome. Perfect meant perfect—

courageous, determined, a brilliant horseman. In other words, perfect.

When the time was right, he, King Humphrey III, would go on a quest for the lad.

Two

When Cinderellis was old enough to start farming, his brothers gave him the rockiest acres to work, the acres that went halfway up Biddle Mountain, the acres with the caves he loved to explore.

"It's a small section," Burt said, "but you're no farmer, Cinderellis."

"Not like us," Ralph said. He smiled his special smile at Burt, the smile that made Cinderellis ache with longing.

"Do we have any popping corn?" Cinderellis asked, excited. This was his big chance to prove he *was* a farmer. Then Ralph and Burt would smile the special smile at him too.

He took the popping corn and mixed it with flying powder and extra-strength powder. Then he stuffed the mixture under the biggest rocks on his acres. He added twigs and lit them.

The corn popped extra high. The rocks burst out of the ground and rolled to the bottom of the mountain. The soil became light and soft and ready for planting. Cinderellis mixed his seeds with growing powder and planted them. Then he set up an invention workshop in his biggest cave.

At harvesttime Cinderellis couldn't wait for his brothers to see his vegetables. His carrots were sweeter than maple syrup. His tomatoes were redder than red paint. And his potatoes were so beautiful, you could hardly look at them. Ralph and Burt would have to admit he was a farmer.

Cinderellis sprinkled balancing powder on his vegetables and loaded them on his wheelbarrow. Then he pushed the wheelbarrow to the barn without losing even a single ruby-red radish.

Ralph and Burt were still in the fields, so Cinderellis arranged his vegetables outside the barn door. Using more balancing powder and a pinch of extra-strength powder, he stacked the tomatoes in the shape of a giant tomato and the beets in the shape of a giant beet. His masterpiece was the carrots, rising like a ballerina from a tiny tiny tip.

Finally his brothers drove up in the wagon behind Thelma the mule.

Burt took one look and said, "Tomatoes are too red."

Ralph tasted a carrot and said, "Carrots are too sweet."

9

HIS MASTERPIECE WAS THE CARROTS, RISING
LIKE A BALLERINA FROM A TINY TINY TIP.

Burt added, "Potatoes are too pretty."

Cinderellis said, "But carrots should taste sweet, and tomatoes are supposed to be red." He shouted, "And what's wrong with pretty potatoes?"

Ralph said, "Guess I'll load them on the wagon anyway."

Burt said, "Might as well take them to market."

Cinderellis left them there. He went to his workshop and screamed.

⚓ ⚓ ⚓

When Marigold was seven and a half, King Humphrey III left Biddle Castle again, to go on a quest for water from the well of youth and happiness. Marigold missed him terribly. She told Apricot how miserable she was. Apricot purred happily. He loved it when his dear lass talked to him, and he was sure it meant she was in a good mood.

Marigold patted the cat. Apricot was wonderful, but she wished for a human friend, someone who would understand her feelings, someone who would rather be home with her than be anywhere else in the world.

⚓ ⚓ ⚓

It was the end of the first day of fall, and Cinderellis was nine years old. He woke up exactly at midnight because his bed had begun to shake. On the bureau the jars of his wake-up powder and no-smell-hose powder jiggled and rattled.

But as soon as he got up to see what was going on, the shaking stopped. So he went back to sleep.

In the morning Ralph and Burt and Cinderellis discovered that the grass in their best hay field had vanished.

A tear trickled down Ralph's cheek. "Goblins did it," he said.

Burt nodded, wiping his eyes.

Cinderellis walked across the brown field. Huh! he thought. Look at that! Hoofprints! He picked up a golden hair. "It was a horse with a golden mane," he announced. "Not goblins."

His brothers didn't listen. Ralph knelt and poured dirt from his left hand into his right. Burt poured dirt from his right hand into his left. Cinderellis got down on his knees too. Although he didn't see what good it would do, he poured dirt from his left hand into his right. Then he poured it from his right hand into his left.

Ralph said, "Get up, Cinderellis. Don't be such a copycat."

Cinderellis stood, feeling silly. And lonelier than ever.

Three

During the winter after the hay disappeared, King Humphrey III returned. He hadn't found the well of youth and happiness, but he'd brought home a flask of coconut milk that was supposed to be just as good.

The milk didn't make anyone a day younger or a smile happier, though. All it did was make people's toenails grow, a foot an hour. This kept the Chief Royal Manicurist busy for a week, till the effects wore off.

Marigold waited for her turn with the manicurist in the throne room with her father and all the nobles who'd had a sip of the milk. Everyone's boots and hose were off, and the smell made Apricot sneeze on his cushion next to Marigold's chair.

Marigold didn't mind the smell. She was too happy about seeing her father to mind anything—until he mentioned that he was planning a new quest, this time for a pair of seven-league boots.

Marigold would have left the room, if she had been able to walk with three-foot-long toenails. As it was, everybody saw her cry.

⚓ ⚓ ⚓

A year to the day after the hay vanished, Cinderellis' farmhouse shook again in the middle of the night. In the morning the hay was gone again from the same field, and Cinderellis picked up another horse hair, a copper one.

Every night for the next year, Ralph practiced a spell to scare away the goblins.

Goblins, go away *NOW!*
Go go go go *GO!*
Away away away away *AWAY!*
Now now now now *NOW!*

"The words are hard to remember," Ralph said.

Burt agreed. "Almost impossible."

Even though he knew that goblins had nothing to do with the disappearing hay, Cinderellis wanted to help. So he invented goblin-stay-away powder. It was made of dried vinegar and the claw of a dead eagle, the two things goblins fear most.

The first day of fall came. At night Ralph headed for the barn, which was right behind the hay field. He'd wait there for the goblins and say the spell.

"Let me come along," Cinderellis said. "I'll bring my goblin-stay-away powder."

"Don't need you," Ralph said. He smiled his special smile at Burt.

Burt smiled back. "What good would you be?" he asked.

In the middle of the night Cinderellis was still awake, because he was having imaginary conversations with his brothers, conversations in which they were amazed at how wonderful his inventions were. Conversations in which they begged him to be their friend.

At midnight the ground shook. Cinderellis smiled. Now Ralph would see that he, Cinderellis, had been right all along. Now Ralph would see the horse.

The next morning Ralph was already eating his oatmeal when Burt and Cinderellis sat down for breakfast.

"Hay all right?" Burt asked.

Ralph shook his head. "Rain today."

"Have to get the corn in," Burt said. "What happened?"

"Ground shook. Said the spell. Went to sleep. Hay was gone."

"Did you see the horse?" Cinderellis asked.

"What horse?"

"Didn't you look outside the barn?"

Ralph smiled at Burt. "What for?"

Burt guffawed.

Later that day Cinderellis found a silver horse's hair in the hay field.

The following year it was Burt's turn to spend the night in the barn. In the morning the hay was gone.

"My turn next," Cinderellis said, picking up a golden horse hair from the bare field.

Ralph and Burt roared with laughter.

"My turn next," Cinderellis insisted, turning red. He'd save the hay. His brothers would admire him at last. And he'd never be lonely again.

❖ ❖ ❖

A month after Burt's night in the barn, King Humphrey III returned to Biddle without finding the seven-league boots. What he had found were three shoes that walked backward, very slowly. They went straight to the Royal Museum of Quest Souvenirs.

Marigold asked her father when he would go off on his next quest. He said he was leaving in three days to find the lark whose song is sweeter than harp music.

Marigold nodded sadly and went to her bedchamber, where she patted Apricot's head and thought gloomy thoughts. Apricot closed his eyes, glad that his dear lass was happy.

Cats are so loyal, Marigold thought, swallowing her tears. They never go off on quests. They never leave you alone and lonely.

Four

Cinderellis spent day after day in his workshop cave, getting ready for the horse's arrival. He needed something to keep it from grazing, so he invented horse treats. They were made of oats and molasses and a few other ingredients to make the treats particularly scrumptious to horses—ground horse chestnuts, minced horse mackerel, and chopped horse nettles.

And since horses are partial to apples, Cinderellis made the treats apple shaped. He tried them out on Thelma and she liked them, even though she was a mule. Horses would adore them.

After he'd perfected the treats, Cinderellis turned one of his caves into a stable—an unusual stable, where the water trough refilled itself from a rain barrel outside the cave, where the rock floor had been softened by fluffy powder, and where there were paintings of subjects that horses like. Cinderellis had done the paintings himself. One was a close-up of three blades of spring grass. Another was of the ground as it would look to a galloping horse. And the last was of trees as they'd look to a cantering horse.

It was a lot of effort for just one night—because after that Ralph and Burt would probably keep the horse in the barn with Thelma. But Cinderellis didn't mind. It would be worth everything if he could be friends with his brothers. A little extra work didn't matter compared to that.

✢ ✢ ✢

In the middle of the summer King Humphrey III returned from his quest. But instead of the lark that sings more sweetly than a harp, he brought home a mule whose bray drowns out an orchestra.

A week later, the king left on a quest for the goose that lays golden eggs.

Marigold noticed that the other castle children were laughing at the latest quest souvenir. Whenever she and Apricot approached a group of them, they'd be braying as hard as they could. When they saw her, they'd run away, giggling.

Marigold wished she could be a part of their group and laugh along with them. The king's souvenirs *were* funny. They would make her laugh too, if she had someone to laugh with.

⚓ ⚓ ⚓

Late at night after the first day of fall, Cinderellis snuck out to the barn with a bucket of horse treats. A little before midnight he heard distant hoofbeats. He opened the barn door a crack. The grass was still there.

The hoofbeats grew louder. The floorboards hummed. The hoofbeats grew even louder. The rafters hummed along with the floorboards. Cinderellis' hands shook and his teeth rattled.

Then the shaking stopped. A coppercolored mare stepped into the field. She was the biggest, most beautiful horse Cinderellis had ever seen. Across her back lay a knight in copper armor.

SHE WAS THE BIGGEST, MOST BEAUTIFUL
HORSE CINDERELLIS HAD EVER SEEN.
ACROSS HER BACK LAY A KNIGHT IN COPPER ARMOR.

This was a surprise. Cinderellis hadn't expected anyone to be on the horse.

The mare lowered her head and started to graze.

She mustn't do that! Cinderellis thought. He grabbed the bucket of horse treats and left the barn.

The horse looked up and saw an ordinary farm lad, but she liked his face. He could rescue her from the evil magician who had put a spell on her and her two sisters. The lad only had to touch her bridle and she'd be safe. The spell would be broken, and she wouldn't have to return to the magician ever again. She let the lad come right up to her. Touch the bridle, she thought. Touch the bridle.

He held out the horse treats.

She sniffed the bucket. Mmm,

pleasant. She put her head in the bucket and started to munch. Yum, delectable. And the treats were shaped like apples. Great combination!

Take the bridle, lad. Please!

Cinderellis grabbed the bridle. I've got you now, he thought.

Aah! The mare was so happy. She loved this lad. She would do anything for him.

Cinderellis put the bucket down and tiptoed to the knight lying across the mare's back. "Sir, are you all right?"

The knight didn't move.

"Sir?" Cinderellis raised his voice. "Sir? Can you hear me?"

The knight didn't answer.

Cinderellis tapped the metal. "Excuse me, sir. I hope you don't mind . . ."

Nothing.

He tapped louder. It sounded hollow.

He lifted the couter, which covered the knight's elbow. It felt too light. If an arm were in there, it would be heavier. The knight was just an empty suit of armor! And he'd been talking to it!

Five

Cinderellis led the mare to the stable cave. Inside, he lifted the armor off her back and dumped it behind a mound of hay. He took her saddle and bridle off too. Then he began to brush her.

It felt sooo good. She whinnied softly.

What should he call her? He wanted a name that meant something.

He had it. Chasam. It stood for Copper Horse Arrives Shortly After Midnight. He picked up a handful of oats and fed it to her. "Good night, Chasam."

In the morning Cinderellis led his

brothers to the hay field.

"See," he said. "I saved it."

Burt said, "Goblin spell worked after all." He smiled the special smile at Ralph.

It wasn't the spell!

Ralph smiled back. He said, "Just took a while."

"It wasn't the spell," Cinderellis hollered. "I did it!"

"Time to gather the hay," Ralph said.

Cinderellis opened his mouth to tell them about Chasam and then shut it again. What if he told them and they still wouldn't admit he'd done anything? What if they said a goblin had run away because of the spell, but his horse had stayed? That was probably what they would say! And once they saw Chasam, they'd keep her for themselves. They'd never let him have a turn riding her or plowing with her.

Well, he wasn't telling them. Chasam would be his secret. He'd let them have next year's horse—*if* they admitted that he had saved the field. He'd let them have all the horses if they'd be his friends. After all, friends don't hold out on each other.

To get his mind off his brothers, Cinderellis spent the day with Chasam. He rode her, which was nothing like riding Thelma the mule, or even like riding the horses at the yearly fair in Snettering-on-Snoakes. Those horses weren't as tall as Chasam was. So tall you were higher than anybody and felt more important too. And their gaits weren't silken like hers. She hardly jiggled, even when she trotted. And her gallop was completely thrilling. The trees whizzed by, and the breeze that had ruffled Cinderellis' hair when he started out—that breeze was miles behind. Why, he almost caught up to yesterday's thunderstorm.

After an hour Cinderellis dismounted and started tossing horse treats to Chasam. He'd throw them, and she'd run after them and gobble them up. Sometimes she'd catch them before they landed. As time went on she became better and better, till she could catch almost anything he could throw.

It was fun, but he couldn't spend every minute playing, so he stopped and got busy. His drying powder wasn't quite right, and there had been a lot of rain lately. His lettuces were drowning.

He let Chasam graze while he did his experiments. He added ingredients that kept out water—ground umbrella, diced hood of a poncho, and pulverized roof shingle.

Chasam came over and watched.

At least someone's interested in me and my inventions, Cinderellis thought. Even if it's only a horse.

⚓ ⚓ ⚓

Two days before Marigold's thirteenth birthday King Humphrey III returned from his latest quest, bringing with him the turkey that lays tin eggs.

A week later the king mounted his horse in the castle courtyard. He was leaving again, this time to search for the lamp that commands a genie. Marigold begged him not to go.

King Humphrey III reached down and stroked her forehead. "But sweetheart," he said, "wouldn't you like a genie who would make all your wishes come true?"

Apricot squirmed in Marigold's arms. That horse's head was bigger than his whole body. He wanted his dear lass to step away from the horse.

Marigold shrugged. Sure she'd like a genie, so she could wish for her father to stop going on quests. But if he'd just stop on his own, she wouldn't need a genie. Besides, the king would never actually bring back a genie, so what was the point of wanting one?

Six

Late at night, a year after Chasam's arrival, Cinderellis and the mare waited in the hay field. Cinderellis had a pail of horse treats with him. At a few minutes before midnight Chasam started neighing and running in circles.

At midnight the ground began to tremble. Cinderellis' hands shook. The earth shimmied and lurched. Cinderellis' teeth rattled. The trees swayed and twisted. The hay field churned and pitched. Cinderellis' stomach sloshed.

Then everything grew quiet. A silver mare stepped into the hay field. A suit of silver armor lay across her back. Cinderellis felt disloyal thinking it, but the silver horse was even more beautiful than Chasam. Bigger, stronger, and just a little prettier around her eyes.

Chasam galloped to the mare. They nuzzled. They raced together across the field. They reared up and batted each other playfully with their front hooves. Then, at last, they trotted to Cinderellis and stood by him, their sides heaving.

Cinderellis grabbed the silver mare's bridle. The silver mare was overjoyed. She loved this farm lad and would do anything for him.

"Welcome, Shasam," Cinderellis said. Shasam stood for Silver Horse Arrives Shortly After Midnight. He led her to the stable cave. Inside, he lifted off her armor and tossed it on top of the copper armor.

In the morning Cinderellis showed Ralph and Burt that the hay field was all right.

Ralph said, "Goblins didn't come back."

Burt said, "Good year for turnips." He put his arm across Ralph's shoulder. They walked to the barn, leaving Cinderellis standing by himself.

He swallowed the lump in his throat. He wasn't going to give Shasam to his brothers either.

She was even more fun to ride than Chasam. Faster, smoother, *mightier*. She was better at catching horse treats too. But Cinderellis didn't want to hurt Chasam's feelings, so he pretended he never noticed the difference.

✤ ✤ ✤

The following June King Humphrey III
returned home. Instead of finding the
lamp that commands a genie, he had
stumbled over the candle that rouses
an imp. The imp was so angry about
being bothered that he put a curse on
the king—King Humphrey III had to
go home and stay there. No quests for
five whole years.

The king was heartbroken. His next
quest was going to be the most important one ever. Marigold was old enough
to get married, and he'd planned to
find the perfect lad for her. And now he
couldn't.

Marigold was sorry her father was
unhappy, but she was delighted that he
was going to stay home. She was also
delighted that he couldn't search for

her husband. It would be awful to have to marry something he brought back from a quest.

Apricot noticed the king weeping, and he worried that his dear lass might be sad too.

The day after he returned, King Humphrey III sat in the throne room and tried to listen to his Royal Councillors, but he couldn't concentrate. Without a quest, how was he going to find the right husband for his darling daughter?

Then he had a brilliant thought. If he couldn't go searching for the right lad, he'd make lots of lads come to him! But how would he know which one was perfect? Hmm. He began to have an idea.

⚓ ⚓ ⚓

Exactly a year after Shasam's arrival, Chasam, Shasam, and Cinderellis waited in the hay meadow for Ghasam (Golden Horse Arrives Shortly After Midnight).

Half an hour before midnight, the wind picked up. Cinderellis felt a tremor. And another. The wind howled.

Midnight came. The ground rocked and bucked. The wind went wild, blowing from every direction. A tree was uprooted and sailed away into the east. Cinderellis' hands shook, his teeth rattled, and his stomach sloshed.

The world went black. The moon had gone out! The stars had gone out! Cinderellis' heart bounced up and down.

Then the wind stopped. The ground steadied. The moon and stars reappeared.

A golden horse stepped into the hay field. A suit of golden armor lay across her back. Cinderellis gasped. She was gorgeous. You looked at her, and you heard trumpets playing and cymbals crashing.

Chasam and Shasam nickered. They cantered to their sister and nuzzled her. Then all three galloped joyously around the hay field, legs flying, necks stretched out, their manes and tails streaming.

Finally they stopped, and Ghasam trotted to Cinderellis. She whinnied as he took her bridle. She loved this farm lad already. She'd do anything for him.

The next morning Cinderellis told Burt and Ralph that the hay would never disappear again. He held his breath and waited. If they thanked him and smiled the special smile at him, then they could have Ghasam.

Ralph said, "Wet weather coming."

Burt said, "Maybe some hail."

Cinderellis breathed out. Nothing had changed. So he'd keep the horses, and he'd have three loyal and true animal friends. Who needed human friends anyway?

Seven

Ghasam was better than her sisters
at catching horse treats. And she was
faster than they were too. Once, when
Cinderellis jumped on her back, he
started to sneeze. "A—" he said. She
took off. He finished the sneeze.
"Choo!" They had gone two miles.

When they got back to the stable
cave after that gallop, Cinderellis told
Ghasam what a phenomenal horse
she was. Then he told Chasam and
Shasam what phenomenal horses they
were, because he didn't want them to

feel left out. He knew only too well what that was like.

⚜ ⚜ ⚜

Princess Marigold turned fifteen. There were banquets and balls and puppet shows in her honor. Everyone said she was the sweetest, kindest, least uppity princess in the world. And pretty to boot.

Nobody mentioned that she was also the most terrified princess, because she had told only Apricot about that, and he had misunderstood anyway.

She was scared because of her father and his—well, his crazy ideas. Since he couldn't go on a quest, he had devised a contest to find her future husband. He hadn't revealed the contest rules yet, but he had said that the winner would be courageous, determined, and a fine horseman. Considering the king's

44

quest souvenirs, though, Marigold thought she'd probably wind up marrying a mean stubborn gnome who could ride kangaroos!

The final banquet was almost over when King Humphrey III stood and beamed at his guests. "Dear friends," he began. "Tomorrow our Royal Glassworkers will begin to create a giant hill in the shape of a pyramid. It will be made entirely of glass. When it is completed, our darling daughter will wait at the top with a basket of golden apples. The brave lad who rides his horse up to her and takes three apples will have her hand in marriage."

Marigold fainted. Her father was too excited to notice. Except for Apricot, nobody noticed. They were too astonished. Apricot was worried. Had his dear lass eaten something that disagreed with her?

King Humphrey III continued. "We will also give the provinces of Skiddle, Luddle, and Buffle to the winner to rule immediately. And he will be king of all of Biddle after I'm gone. Any lad can compete. All he needs is a horse and a suit of armor."

After she recovered from her faint, Marigold tried to persuade her father to change his mind. But he wouldn't listen. He said the winner of the contest would be perfect for her and perfect for Biddle.

Marigold disagreed. The man who won the contest would be cruel and evil. No kind person would make a horse climb a glass hill.

And she would have to marry him.

⚜ ⚜ ⚜

In a week the pyramid was built. Its glass was clearer than a drop of dew and slipperier than the sides of an ice cube. King Humphrey III wasn't completely satisfied, though, because it was level on top. But Marigold had flatly refused to sit on a point.

The pyramid's actual point was made by a cloth canopy that would be over the princess's head, giving her shade. King Humphrey III sighed. It would have to do.

The king announced the contest in a proclamation. Cinderellis heard about it from Ralph at breakfast. Not because Ralph told him. No. Ralph told Burt. Naturally.

"The contest starts tomorrow." Ralph laughed. "Burt, do you think Thelma wants to climb a glass hill?"

Burt laughed for five minutes

straight. "That's funny," he said.

Ralph said, "Want to see it?"

Burt said, "Wouldn't miss it."

They didn't ask me if I want to see it with them, Cinderellis thought. Well, he didn't. He wanted to climb the pyramid. He wondered how slippery the glass was.

Cinderellis didn't want to become a prince and marry a princess he'd never even met. He just wanted to see if his sticky powder would take him and one of the mares up the glass hill. And then he wanted to show the golden apples to Ralph and Burt. They were giving up a day of farming to see the contest. That meant they cared about it. And they'd love the golden apples. They were farmers, after all. They loved fruit. When Cinderellis gave the apples to them, they'd love him too.

He took some sticky powder from his

room and started walking toward
Biddle Castle.

✤ ✤ ✤

Dressed as a Royal Dairymaid, Princess
Marigold wandered through the field
around the pyramid. She passed gaily
colored tents and neighing, stamping
horses and shouting, striding knights
and squires. There are hundreds of
contestants, she thought. And not
one of them had even asked to meet
her. All they wanted was to rule Skiddle,
Luddle, and Buffle. And to make their
poor horses go up a stupid glass hill.

But perhaps there was one man
among them who would be a good ruler,
even if he didn't care about her. Maybe
he had an extraordinary horse who
didn't mind trying to climb glass, a
horse so well treated that it would do

anything for its rider.

If such a man was here, she had to find him and figure out how to get him to the top.

She squared her shoulders. To find him, she had to talk to all of them, all the horse torturers. That was why she had dressed as a Royal Dairymaid and left Apricot in the castle—so no one would suspect she was a princess.

⚓ ⚓ ⚓

Cinderellis saw the glass hill from a mile and a half away, sparkling in the sunlight. It was as high and almost as steep as the castle's highest tower. When he got close, he saw the Royal Guards surrounding the pyramid. He knew one of them—Farley, who used to sell candy apples at the yearly fair in Snettering-on-Snoakes.

Cinderellis asked Farley to let him touch the glass hill. Farley looked around to make sure nobody was watching. Then he nodded.

Cinderellis barely felt the hill because his hand slipped off so fast. For a second it felt lovely—cool and smoother than smooth. And then his hand was back at his side. He tried again. Mmm, pleasant. Whoops!

"A lot of people are here, aren't they?" Cinderellis said.

Farley turned to look at the crowd. Quickly, Cinderellis tossed a handful of sticky powder on the hill.

"Yup," Farley said.

Three quarters of the powder rolled off the hill! If sticky powder, which stuck to *everything*, rolled off, then that hill was the slipperiest thing Cinderellis had ever seen, felt, or imagined.

Eight

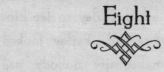

Princess Marigold hadn't talked to a single contestant who would be a good ruler. Some wanted to raise taxes. Some wanted to have hunting parties all the time. One even said he'd declare war and take over all of Biddle! Another said he'd drown Apricot, because he didn't want cat hair all over everything! If either of them reached the top of the hill, she'd kick him all the way to the bottom. She'd *swallow* the golden apples before she'd let either of them get his hands on them.

After talking to at least a hundred

contestants, Marigold gave up. She just stared at the pyramid, trying not to bawl.

Cinderellis stared at it too. He imagined climbing it while Ralph and Burt watched.

He said good-bye to Farley and backed into a person behind him. "Oops! Excuse me." He turned around.

He'd bumped into a Royal Dairymaid. A pretty one, with a sweet face, a very sweet face.

Now here's someone with a kind face, Marigold thought. Too bad he was a farm lad. It would be a waste of time to talk to him, since he wouldn't have a suit of armor. But she wanted to know what someone who looked so kind would say.

She smiled at him, feeling shy because he looked so nice. "Er, pardon me. What would you do if you won the contest and became prince of Skiddle and Luddle and Buffle?"

He liked her dimple. "What?" What had she said? "Sorry."

None of the others had apologized for anything. "That's all right." She repeated the question.

"I don't know." He wished he had a good answer. "I don't want to be a prince."

Ah. What a good answer. "But if you had to be?"

He wondered why she wanted to know. But why not? He was curious about lots of things too. "I guess if I were prince, I'd create inventions that would make my subjects' lives easier." That's right. That's what he *would* do. What could he invent for a Royal Dairymaid? "For example, I'd invent

"I DON'T KNOW." HE WISHED HE HAD A GOOD
ANSWER. "I DON'T WANT TO BE A PRINCE."

cow treats." He nodded, figuring it out. He'd leave out the special horse ingredients and add some ground cow parsnip and dried cow shark instead. "The cows would love the treats, and they'd love to be milked."

"That would be a great invention," the princess said. He wanted to do something that animals would like! This lad would never torture a horse.

Nobody had ever encouraged Cinderellis before. She was the nicest maiden in Biddle. "I already invented horse treats," he said, boasting a little.

"They must be delicious," Marigold said. Gosh! she thought, he's already done something to make horses happy. "Um," she added, "if you did become a prince, would you go on quests?"

Cinderellis shook his head. "When I want something, I invent it, or invent a way to get it." He added in a rush, "Most of my inventions are powders that do things." He stopped. "You're probably not interested."

"I am! Please tell me about them." If she knew him better, they might be friends—her first human friend.

"Well, my first invention was flying powder." He told her about the powders.

She listened and asked questions. Cinderellis had never had so much fun in his life. This Royal Dairymaid was splendid!

Marigold had never had so much fun either. She especially liked the idea of fluffy powder. You'd always have a soft place to sit, and—oh my! "Your fluffy powder could save lives. If a person—or, say, a cat—fell out of a window, you could sprinkle fluffy powder on the ground. And the cat wouldn't be hurt." She beamed at him.

He beamed back. "I'm thinking of using my sticky powder—"

"Oh no!" Marigold saw the king heading their way. "I'd better go. I have some milking to do." She curtsied and fled into the crowd.

"Where do you . . . When could I . . ."

But she was gone, and he didn't even know her name.

Nine

Back in his workshop cave, Cinderellis got to work. Sticky powder alone
wouldn't get him up the glass hill, so
he mixed in extra-strength powder and
a few other ingredients. While he
invented, he thought about the Royal
Dairymaid. He wished he'd had a
chance to tell her he was going to climb
the pyramid. Then she could have
watched and rooted for him.

But she might have thought he
wanted to marry the princess. He
didn't. He wanted— He stopped mixing. He wanted to marry the Royal

Dairymaid! He hadn't felt lonely for a second while they'd talked.

But he didn't know her name, so how could he marry her? Well, she was a Royal Dairymaid, so he should be able to find her again. There couldn't be that many of them.

Suppose he didn't show the golden apples to Ralph and Burt. They might like the apples, but they probably wouldn't be interested in his special sticky powder, since they never cared about his inventions, not one bit. So suppose he hid the apples instead, till the princess married somebody else. Then suppose he sold them and used the money to set up an invention workshop in Snettering-on-Snoakes. He'd do what he'd said a prince should do— invent things to make people's lives easier. He'd sell his inventions, and he'd marry the Royal Dairymaid.

He started mixing again. Yes, he'd marry her. That is, if she'd have him.

The powder was ready to try out. He spread it on Ghasam's front hoof.

She couldn't lift her foot. She strained. Finally she forced it up—with grass and dirt attached.

Too strong. He cleaned off her hoof. Then he added a pinch of this and a teaspoon of that and spread the mixture on Shasam's hooves.

Now the powder didn't work at all. Shasam could even gallop. He frowned. Maybe his on-off powder was in the "off" phase when her feet were on the ground and in the "on" phase when her feet were in the air. That would mean that the sticky powder was only active when there was nothing to stick to.

He could fix that. He tapped each

THE POWDER WAS READY TO TRY OUT.

hoof with a stick. That should reset the phases.

There. Each step was difficult, and Shasam had to strain a little to lift her hooves, but she could lift them and the grass and dirt didn't come up too. Good.

Now he needed to add his time-release powder, which would turn the stickiness on when they started climbing the glass hill and turn it off when they got back to the bottom.

↯ ↯ ↯

Marigold woke up in the middle of the night. She had dreamed of a secret weapon that would keep a horse and rider from getting to the top of the glass hill. With her secret weapon she wouldn't have to marry someone who was mean and nasty and cruel. She patted Apricot, who was curled up next to her, and fell back to sleep, smiling.

Early the next morning Royal Servants climbed a ladder to the top of the pyramid. They brought with them an outdoor throne, a picnic lunch for a princess and a cat, the basket of golden apples, and a water bowl for Apricot. When they came down, Marigold carried Apricot and the secret weapon to the top. As soon as she got there, the Royal Servants took the ladder away and the contest began.

❧ ❧ ❧

After breakfast the same morning, Ralph said, "Good day to watch a glass hill." He guffawed.

Burt guffawed.

Ralph pushed back his chair and walked out of the farmhouse. Burt pushed back his chair and followed

him. Cinderellis wondered if the Royal
Dairymaid would be watching the
contest.

At the workshop cave, he worked on
his powder some more. Finally he
thought it was ready.

⚓ ⚓ ⚓

At first Marigold had been ready with
her secret weapon whenever a horse
galloped at the pyramid. But rider after
rider failed to climb up even one inch,
so she relaxed and became interested
in looking down on everything. The
knights and squires seemed no bigger
than her hand, and their cries and the
neighing of their horses sounded muf-
fled and thin. Only Biddle Mountain
appeared as big as ever, looming in the
distance, much higher than the glass
hill.

The day grew warmer and Marigold grew hot—hot and bored. Apricot was hot too, but he knew his dear lass had brought him up there to show everyone how important he was to her. So he rubbed himself against her leg and purred.

Marigold wished she knew the name of the nice farm lad. Even if she never saw him again, though, she'd remember their conversation forever.

✿ ✿ ✿

Cinderellis wanted to scream. He'd been putting the copper suit of armor on for hours. He'd finally gotten the tasset and the mail skirt on over his waist and hips. The cuisses and the poleyns and the greaves were on his legs. The sabatons were on his feet. The vambraces were on his arms. The couters were over his elbows.

But the breastplate kept popping off!

Over and over he'd hammered it here and bent it there. And it would hold— for about ten seconds. Then—*POP!*

At this rate he'd never get to the pyramid.

Ten

A knight on a black stallion prepared to climb the hill. The stallion looked bigger than any of the other horses. Marigold reached for her secret weapon.

But the stallion's hooves slipped off the pyramid as soon as they touched it. The knight made the horse try again—and the horse slipped again. The knight wanted to try a third time, but everybody yelled that he should let the rest of them take a turn.

Burt and Ralph laughed so hard, their sides hurt.

Marigold put her secret weapon down

and started breathing again. It was three thirty. Only a few more hours till it would be too dark to see the hill and she could come down. Only a few more hours and it would be over forever.

But then her father would come up with another horrible plan.

❧ ❧ ❧

Cinderellis had finally wedged the breastplate under the fauld. And he'd managed to mount Chasam, even though it had taken over an hour. He'd picked Chasam because she'd looked so disappointed when he'd tried the powder out on Ghasam.

He pulled the gauntlets over his hands. Now for the helmet. Uh-oh. He couldn't make his hands in the gauntlets do anything. He'd never get the helmet on. He took the gauntlets off again and put the helmet on.

Now he couldn't see to put on the
gauntlets. He could only see through
one chink in the visor, just enough to
steer Chasam.

Well, he didn't need to see. He could
feel. There. The gauntlets were on.

Now where were the reins? He
couldn't tell through the gauntlets.
Were these the reins? He hoped so.

He kicked Chasam, harder than he
meant to. She didn't mind. They were
off. It was five o'clock.

⚓ ⚓ ⚓

Two more horses to go. Marigold
scratched under her tiara. She felt hot
and sticky. Apricot was drinking from
his water bowl. She was glad he was
up here with her. She wished that kind
farm lad were here too. She'd introduce

him to Apricot, and he'd invent something nice for a cat.

One more horse to go.

Marigold wondered what her father
would dream up next. Maybe he'd
make her sit at the bottom of a glass
hole, and the horse that didn't crash
down and squash her would have her
hand and Skiddle, Luddle, and Buffle.

The last horse, like the 213 before it,
failed to climb the hill. Marigold stood
up. At last. She hadn't needed her
secret weapon. Wait! What was that?
A cloud of dust coming from Biddle
Mountain?

In the field below, King Humphrey
III couldn't see the dust cloud. He
decided that the contestants could all
try again tomorrow. He didn't want to
end the contest after just one day when
it was so important.

Then he heard people shouting. There was another rider? Let him come, then. Maybe this one would be enough of a horseman to climb the pyramid. Maybe this one deserved Marigold.

Cinderellis saw the pyramid through the chink in the visor. They were almost there.

Everyone was astonished at the beauty and size of the copper-colored mare. Everyone was also amazed that such a glorious horse would let herself be ridden by that nutty knight or whatever he was. For one thing, his armor was tarnished and filthy. His posture was terrible. His hands and the reins were flopping around in his lap. He wasn't even really riding the mare. She was carrying him, like cargo.

Marigold's heart started pounding.

Chasam cantered up to the glass hill. Cinderellis sort of kicked her to keep going. She placed her front right hoof on the hill. She leaned her weight on it. It held!

She started to climb. The watching crowd grew silent.

Marigold didn't know what to do. If this mare climbed the hill, it would be because she wanted to. Any fool could see the mare's rider wasn't making her do anything. But the rider still could be mean and nasty. Marigold picked up her secret weapon.

But maybe he's nice, she thought, as nice as the farm lad. She had to find out. At least she had to see his face. "Sir!" she called. "Please take off your helmet."

Who was yelling? Cinderellis could see only the glass hill in front of him.

He tried to look up, but all he saw was the inside of the helmet. Was something wrong? He tried to push his visor up. Nothing happened.

"I'd like to see your face," Marigold called.

Somebody was yelling again. Cinderellis decided to take the helmet completely off. He pushed up on it. Nothing happened.

Chasam was a tenth of the way up the hill. The crowd on the ground almost stopped breathing.

He's trying to do what I want, Marigold thought. That's something. And he didn't force the horse up the hill. She laughed. If he couldn't even get his helmet off, he'd never be able to pick up the apples—if he climbed all the way up.

She thought of tossing the apples

into his lap. If nobody ever got to the top, the next contest could be worse than this one. Or her father might let this contest go on forever, and she'd spend the rest of her life up here.

She put the secret weapon down. The apples were next to the throne. She took one, aimed carefully, and threw. The apple landed on Chasam's saddle, in the little valley between the saddle and Cinderellis' mail skirt.

Huh! Cinderellis thought. Did something hit me?

Marigold picked up another apple. She would have thrown it, but she got worried. She was taking an awful chance. She hadn't seen the knight and she hadn't talked to him. Maybe they could talk, even if she couldn't see him. "Sir," she called, "what would you do if you ruled Skiddle, Luddle, and Buffle?"

"What?" Cinderellis yelled. "What? Speak louder."

A roar came from the helmet. Marigold didn't hear words, just a roar. Whatever was in the armor didn't know how to talk. It could only roar. It was a monster! And she'd given it an apple!

Eleven

Marigold reached for the pitcher that held her secret weapon. But she hesitated. She didn't want to hurt the horse.

Chasam was a third of the way up the hill. And climbing.

The monster would be up here in a minute. She had to do something! She'd try to use only enough to make the mare slide down slowly. She leaned over the edge of her platform and poured a thin stream of olive oil down toward Cinderellis.

Everyone watching wondered why the princess was leaning over the edge of the pyramid. They were too far away to see the pitcher of oil.

The powder wasn't made to withstand olive oil. Chasam started to slip.

Cinderellis thought, We're going down! Is Chasam hurt? What went wrong with the powder?

Chasam couldn't drop Cinderellis. She loved him too much. She spread her legs so she wouldn't topple over and slid down slowly.

Ralph's and Burt's mouths dropped open. What a mare! Any other horse would have fallen on its head, or on top of its rider.

At the bottom of the pyramid Chasam turned around and took off at a gallop.

❦ ❦ ❦

King Humphrey III issued a proclamation announcing that there would be a second and a third chance to climb the glass hill.

⚓ ⚓ ⚓

Cinderellis lay panting in the dirt in front of the workshop cave. Chasam, Ghasam, and Shasam were grazing nearby.

It had taken him a half hour to get his helmet off. Once it was off, he'd used his teeth to tear the gauntlets off his hands. And then he'd squirmed out of everything else.

His powder had failed. He had failed.

Shasam sniffed the golden apple, which had fallen into the parsley patch. Cinderellis picked it up, and Shasam cantered a little ways off, ready for a game of horse-treat catch. But Cinderellis was too depressed for games. Besides, Shasam might break a tooth on the stupid golden apple.

One apple wouldn't buy a work-shop in Snettering-on-Snoakes. He wouldn't be able to marry the Royal Dairymaid on just one apple. He might as well not have it.

Still, he wondered how he'd gotten it. The only explanation he could think of was that the princess had thrown it to him. But why would she?

He stood up and carried the armor and the apple into the cave. He dumped the armor on the heap with the other armor and hid the apple behind an out-cropping of rock. Then he headed to the farmhouse for dinner.

Ralph and Burt were just finishing up.

"Did anyone win the contest?" Cinderellis asked.

"Not today," Ralph said. He smiled his special smile at Burt.

Cinderellis didn't even notice.

"Maybe tomorrow," Burt said.

Tomorrow?

"Or the day after," Ralph said.

He had two more chances!

"There was a beautiful mare," Ralph added.

"Mare's rider was an idiot," Burt said.

"Real idiot," Ralph said.

They both laughed.

"Work to do," Cinderellis said. He ran out of the farmhouse. He had to find out what had gone wrong with his powder. And then he had to fix it.

He'd marry that Royal Dairymaid yet!

In the stable cave he lit a lantern and bent over Chasam's left front hoof. She whinnied and blew warm air across his forehead.

Hmmmm. The hoof looked greasy. Cinderellis touched the greasy spot: He tasted it.

81

Olive oil! They'd used olive oil to make the pyramid slipperier. How could they do that without telling? It wasn't fair.

What would repel olive oil? Drying powder might help, but drying powder worked best on water. Olive pits mixed with drying powder? Olive pits were surrounded by olive oil right there in the olive, and they never became soggy, so they must repel the oil. Yes, that should do it. He ran to the farmhouse pantry for olives and olive oil.

⚓ ⚓ ⚓

In the morning Marigold asked the Chief Royal Cook to refill her secret weapon pitcher. But the Chief Royal Cook was fresh out of olive oil. Marigold said walnut oil would be fine.

In the field around the glass hill the

contestants prepared for the day's trial. A knight painted sticky honey on his horse's hooves. A squire scraped his stallion's shoes to make them rough. Another knight screwed hooks into his mare's shoes.

Outside the workshop cave Cinderellis poured olive oil down a rock that was about as steep as the glass hill. Then he dusted his new powder on Ghasam's hoofs. She started to climb and then slipped. Cinderellis added a little more olive-pit powder and told Ghasam to try again.

⚓ ⚓ ⚓

The knight who had painted honey on his horse's hooves galloped up to the glass hill. His horse tried to step onto the hill but slipped right off.

Marigold petted Apricot. It was going

to be another long, hot day.

Ralph grinned at Burt. Burt grinned at Ralph. It was going to be another fun day.

⚓ ⚓ ⚓

It had taken all morning and almost all afternoon, but Cinderellis' new powder was ready. And Cinderellis was ready, in the silver armor. It had been easier to get into, because he'd learned a few tricks the day before. But being inside was as bad as ever. He could hardly see anything, and his hands were almost useless inside the gauntlets. Still, he was in it, and he was mounted on Shasam. Chasam had earned a rest. He'd ride Ghasam tomorrow if anything went wrong today.

But what could go wrong?

Twelve

The sun was setting behind Biddle Mountain. I didn't need the oil at all today, Marigold thought. But then she saw a dust cloud in the distance. Oh no! Could the mare be coming back? Could the monster be coming back?

People started yelling. "The mare! The mare!"

But it wasn't the copper mare. This horse was a mare, but she was silver and even bigger than the copper mare. One thing was the same, though: The same fool was riding as yesterday. Anyone could see that, even though the rider wore dirty banged-up silver armor instead of dirty banged-up copper armor.

Cinderellis and Shasam reached the pyramid. Shasam started to climb the hill. It wasn't hard. She began to trot.

Marigold was terrified. The mare was halfway up the hill. Where was the walnut oil? She put Apricot down and reached for it. The hem of her gown knocked into the basket that held the apples and sent an apple clattering down the pyramid.

Shasam saw the apple. *Horse treat!* She veered and caught it with her teeth. Then she started climbing again.

Marigold poured the walnut oil. Shasam was two thirds of the way up the glass hill, but when the oil touched her hooves, she started to slip. Oh nooo! She fought, and her hooves beat the glass.

At first Cinderellis thought Shasam was dancing. But no, she was falling. Was she all right? Was she hurt?

Shasam slid down the same way Chasam had. At the bottom she made sure Cinderellis was still in the saddle. Then she galloped away, still holding the golden apple between her teeth.

❧ ❧ ❧

Cinderellis was furious. How could they have switched oils on him?

And what would they use tomorrow?

And how had Shasam gotten a golden apple? He couldn't even guess, and he didn't have time to think about it anyway. He had to figure out how to fix his powder. What he needed was an all-purpose oil repellent. On the farm they grew the nuts and grains for every kind of oil that Biddlers used. What if he ground up the hulls and pits of all of them and added that to the powder? It was a big job, but when he was done, he'd have an all-purpose oil-repellent extra-strength time-release on-off sticky powder that would climb any glass hill anywhere.

Inventing the new powder took all night and most of the next day, but finally it was ready. Cinderellis started putting on the golden armor. It was too big, so he dusted it with shrinking powder. And made it too small. So he dusted it with growing powder. And made it too big. He wasn't used to working in such a rush, and he hated it. He sprinkled on just a little shrinking powder. And made it exactly the way it had been when he started. He was going to bounce around in it, but it would have to do. When the contest was over, he was going to invent better armor.

⚓ ⚓ ⚓

Marigold waited for the dust cloud. Everybody else was waiting too.

And there it was—the dust cloud.

The mare was golden this time, and so splendid she took Marigold's breath away. Why did such a marvelous horse let a monster ride her?

Cinderellis ached all over from crashing into a different part of the armor whenever Ghasam took a step. Not only that, his helmet kept bouncing around too. Sometimes he could see outside pretty well. Sometimes he could just see a little. And sometimes all he could see was the inside of the helmet. Whenever he could see, he pointed Ghasam toward the pyramid and hoped for the best.

They reached the glass hill. Ghasam started climbing. Cinderellis' helmet shifted. All he could see now was gray metal and three rivets.

Marigold didn't waste a second. She went right for her pitcher of oil, which was walnut again. She leaned over the edge of the pyramid and started pouring.

The oil flowed down the hill. It reached the mare, but it didn't stop her. She didn't slip a bit. She just kept climbing.

Marigold dropped the pitcher and picked Apricot up. She petted the cat and trembled. She was going to have to marry the monster.

Cinderellis felt Ghasam climb higher and higher. It's working! he thought. If only he could see.

Ghasam stepped onto the platform and stopped. She didn't like being so high up. She shifted from foot to foot.

Cinderellis wondered why Ghasam had stopped. Were they at the top? Had they made it? He tried to move the helmet so he could see. He banged on it, but it didn't budge. He tried to raise the visor, but it wouldn't budge either. How would he get the third apple if he couldn't see?

Marigold hugged Apricot even tighter. Too tight, the cat thought. He wished that she'd stop squeezing and that the horse would go away.

Marigold screamed, "Stay away from us! I won't marry you!"

Somebody was yelling again. "What?" Cinderellis yelled back.

That sounds like a word, Marigold thought. But what was it? What difference did it make? She yelled, "Go away! Leave us alone!"

"What?"

She got it! It had said, "Cat." It wanted Apricot! The monster wanted Apricot! "I'll never give him up, not even if you torture me."

Ghasam wished her dear lad would tell her what to do. She took a step back and then a step forward. She hated it up here.

"What? What is it? What's happening?" Cinderellis shouted. If only he could see. If only he could hear. If only he could find the apple.

Marigold made out another word. The monster had said "cat" again, and "apple." It was saying she better give it the apple or it would take the cat! She jumped up and down with fear and anger. "You can't have them! Go away!"

Cinderellis shoved at the visor and banged the helmet. *Ping!* It sounded like a rivet popping out, but the visor still wouldn't budge.

Ghasam wanted to go home. She took two steps forward.

It's coming at me! Aaaaa! It's going to get us! It can have the apple. Marigold rushed to the basket and snatched up an apple. Then she darted forward and placed it on the saddle in front of Cinderellis.

Apricot hated being so near a horse. He hissed and shot out a paw.

Ghasam shied back. Cinderellis bounced in the saddle. His helmet snapped back, and he stared at the inside of it where his nose should have been. The visor came off and fell onto the platform, but the visor opening was over his forehead, way above his eyes.

Ghasam shied again. Cinderellis' legs knocked into her sides. He wanted her to leave. At last. She started down the hill. At the bottom she began to gallop.

On top of the pyramid Marigold picked up the golden visor. The monster had gone at last.

But it had three apples.

Thirteen

Every day Cinderellis walked to Biddle Castle. He asked all the Royal Dairymaids about his Royal Dairymaid. Nobody knew her. The Royal Dairymaids swore there was no such person.

What good was it to have the golden apples without his sweet, adorable Royal Dairymaid? No good at all.

⚜ ⚜ ⚜

King Humphrey III waited a week for someone to show up with the golden apples. When no one did, he and his

Royal Pages went from house to house, looking for the lad whose armor matched the golden visor.

Marigold came along. She wanted to be there when they found the monster so she could do something. She didn't know what, but something. She left Apricot home to keep him safe for as long as possible.

Two weeks after the last day of the contest, the king reached Cinderellis' farm.

Ralph was weeding the alfalfa field.

King Humphrey III didn't think the fellow looked brave or determined or at all like son-in-law material, but he asked anyway. "Did you climb the glass hill? And do you have a suit of golden armor and three of the princess' golden apples?" He gestured at Marigold.

Ralph bowed to the king. "Nope."

Burt said the same exact thing when they found him in the barley field.

"Are you two the only ones on the farm?" Marigold asked.

"Yup." Then he remembered. "I mean, nope. We have another brother, Cinderellis, but he didn't go to the contest."

"Where is he?" King Humphrey III asked. Burt pointed to Biddle Mountain.

Cinderellis was outside his workshop cave, inventing armor improvements, when Ghasam whinnied. He turned and saw the king and his attendants heading up the mountain.

Cinderellis picked up the pieces of armor and ran into the cave, shooing the horses in ~~ahead of him. Then he~~ rushed to his tomato patch and started weeding.

The king reached the tomatoes. Cinderellis stood and bowed. Then he stared. The Royal Dairymaid was with him. His heart started racing. What was she doing here?

It was the nice farm lad! Marigold smiled in delight.

Cinderellis wondered why there were jewels on her gown.

"Did you climb the glass hill?" King Humphrey III asked. "And do you have a suit of golden armor and three of the princess' golden apples?" He gestured at Marigold.

She was the princess? "Yes! Yes! I have them! I'll get them!" He ran into the workshop cave.

Marigold thought, He's the monster? How could he be?

Cinderellis came out of the cave, leading Chasam, Shasam, and Ghasam.

In his arms were the golden helmet and the three golden apples. He put everything down and knelt before Marigold. "Will you marry me?"

He was smiling up at her. He still looked nice. But then why had he wanted Apricot? "Why did you try to take Apricot?"

What was she talking about? "What apricot?"

"My Apricot. My cat. I had him with me on top of the glass hill."

Cinderellis started laughing. He put on the helmet, jamming it hard over his head. The visor space was over his forehead again. "I can't see anything," he said.

Marigold laughed too. He sounded like the monster. "Take off the helmet," she said.

She was saying something, but he

couldn't hear what it was. Did she say she'd marry him? He pushed up on the helmet. It wouldn't come off. "It's stuck."

"Yes, I'll marry you."

What did she say?

DID SHE SAY SHE'D MARRY HIM? HE PUSHED UP ON
THE HELMET. IT WOULDN'T COME OFF. "IT'S STUCK."

Epilogue

In three days Cinderellis and Marigold were married.

Ralph and Burt came to the ceremony. As soon as it was over, they smiled their special smile at each other and hurried home to harvest the corn.

Chasam, Shasam, and Ghasam became Marigold's pets, just as Apricot was. The only difference was that the horses couldn't fit on the princess' lap. Apricot got used to the horses and even became friends with them. He liked Cinderellis too, once he was convinced—after a few misunderstandings—that his dear lass was happy with the lad. And he loved Cinderellis' first invention as crown prince: cat treats.

Marigold loved all Cinderellis' inventions. She and Cinderellis celebrated their wedding anniversary every year with a demonstration of his all-purpose sticky powder on the glass hill, which they kept polished just for the purpose.

King Humphrey III resumed his questing when the imp's curse ended. He returned with so many souvenirs that an extra wing had to be added to the Museum of Quest Souvenirs.

Cinderellis never went on a single quest. His only trips were to Skiddle, Luddle, and Buffle, and Marigold always went along. While there, she made so many friends that she was never lonely again.

Cinderellis' wetting powder cured

a drought in Skiddle, and his drying powder worked wonders on the floods of Buffle. What's more, he showed the Luddlites how to use growing powder on their wheat crop. Everyone was so grateful that Cinderellis became the most popular ruler in Biddle history. He was never lonely again either.

And they all lived happily ever after.